FiFi Flurry
AND THE
Sleepy
Snowflake!

WRITTEN BY ELAYNE HEANEY

ILLUSTRATED BY PAULA REEL

To David,
My biggest cheerleader.
xxx

Written and Concept by Elayne Heaney
wonderfullyweatherybooks@gmail.com

Illustrations and Design by Paula Reel
www.reel-illustration.com

Copyedit and proof by Liz Hudson
liz@littleredpen.com

First Printing, 2022

ISBN 978-1-3999-3499-2

Published by Wonderfully Weathery Books
Dublin

wonderfullyweatherybooks@gmail.com
www.wonderfullyweatheyrbooks.com

Fifi Flurry come out to play!
Will you bring us some
snowflakes today?

Will you be breezy and chilly too?
We'll wrap up warm
to play with you!

Meet FIFI FLURRY,
She is a snow-flurry called Fifi.
She lives in a place called
WEATHERVILLE,
when it's COOL
and BREEZY.

HOT CHOC

HOT CHOC

THE
COOL
HOTEL

ROOMS

Welcome to
Weatherville

When AUTUMN is over
and the days get cold,
Fifi Flurry arrives
and WINTER takes hold.

She arrives in a
WHIRLWIND,
with her family in tow,
Filling the skies
with their
SPARKLY SNOW.

Fifi Flurry is **MUM** to all the snowflakes, and carries them round from the moment she **WAKES**.

Fifi is friendly,
DAZZLING
and bright,
and she cares
for her children,
all tiny and white.

They hang on her back,
IN HER HAIR and her tum,
And she parades them about –
she's a very proud mum.

Fifi Flurry and her family bring the 'FREEZE' to Weatherville, and the weather pals enjoy their frosty winter chill.

There's skiing, there's snowboarding, iceskating too, And the clouds all wear scarves so they don't CATCH THE FLU!

Bobby Breeze arrives too
bringing a CHILL to the sky,
He loves chasing the snowflakes
and making them FLY!

He blows out his breath
to push into the air,
And they squeal with DELIGHT
as they spiral here and there.

Each little snowflake is
different to the next,
They all have SIX SIDES,
which is very complex!

DENDRITE

PRISM

COLUMN

There are dendrites,
columns and stellar plates,
With some prisms,
needles and
STAR FLAKES
ON SKATES!

These snowflakes love adventure,
to FLUTTER and GLIDE,
But they have to be careful
to stay near their Mum's side.

The sky above is an awfully big place,
and GETTING LOST IS EASY
in such a wide open space.

One day, while playing
with their pal Bobby Breeze,
Bobby's nose STARTS TO TICKLE
and he lets out a sneeze!

From his mouth
there comes a BLAST OF AIR,
Toppling over a snowflake
sitting in Fifi's hair!

The tiny little SNOWFLAKE
FREE-FALLS through the sky,
Tumbling upside down
and trying not to cry!

Bobby looks on as the
snowflake sails away,
And he SHOUTS OUT for help,
his face turning grey!
Fifi Flurry turns to
investigate the NOISE,
And realises the call
is for one of her boys!
She watches from above
as the little flake FALLS FAST,
Tumbling downwards
from the big, sneezy blast!

Round and round the
snowflake SPIRALS and falls,
Spinning over houses,
buildings and snow covered walls.

The trees all around him
are dusted in snow,
Festooned with
BRIGHT LIGHTS
that sparkle and glow.
It all looks so MAGICAL
to this little flake,
Who's tired from tumbling
and trying to
STAY AWAKE!

When at last he finally
comes to a stop,
He falls right off to sleep,
EXHAUSTED from his drop.

Fifi and family come
as quick as they can,
calling his name out trying
to find the little man!

There they spot him atop
the big CHRISTMAS TREE,
Sleeping soundly on the giant star,
for everyone to see!

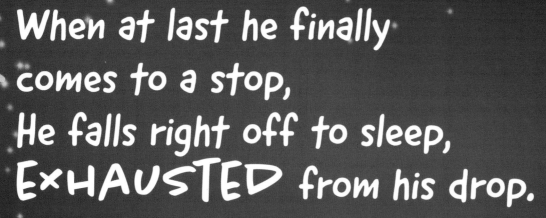

A little girl waves
and shouts out from below,
'LOOK AT THE
CHRISTMAS STAR,
IT'S SPARKLY
WITH SNOW!'
The little flake awakens
from all of the noise,
And hears the CHEERS
from the little girls
and boys.

Who'd have thought
his tumble would bring
so much glee,
When he JUST TOOK A NAP
on a big Christmas tree!

From then, Christmas
became the snowflakes
favourite time of year,

and they loved visiting Earth
bringing their SPARKLE
AND CHEER!

FACTS ABOUT SNOW!

WHAT IS SNOW?

Snow is made of billions of tiny ice crystals that form when the water vapour in the air freezes and form ice crystals – these ice crystals then attach to bits of dirt in the air to form snowflakes! Each snowflake has about 100 or more ice crystals – Wow!

COOL FACTS ABOUT SNOW

- Snow isn't white – is actually clear!
- All snowflakes have 6 sides or arms.
- No two snowflakes are exactly alike.
- Snowflake shapes have lots of different names like Stars, Columns, Needles, Dendrites , Prisms and Stellar Plates to name a few.
- It takes about 1 hour for a snowflake to reach the ground!
- A light snow shower is called a 'SNOW FLURRY'.
- Heavy snowfalls are often called 'SNOWSTORMS'.
- Snowstorms with high winds are called 'BLIZZARDS'.